CHRIS HIGGINS

TROUBLE ON THE FARM

BLOOMSBURY CHILDREN'S BOOKS
Bloomsbury Publishing Plc
50 Bedford Square, London, WC1B 3DP, UK

BLOOMSBURY, BLOOMSBURY CHILDREN'S BOOKS and the Diana logo
are trademarks of Bloomsbury Publishing Plc

First published in Great Britain in 2018 by Bloomsbury Publishing Plc

A catalogue record for this book is available from the British Library

ISBN: PB: 978-1-4088-6887-4; eBook: 978-1-4088-6888-1

2 4 6 8 10 9 7 5 3 1

Printed and bound in Great Britain by CPI Group (UK) Ltd, Croydon CR0 4YY

MIX
Paper from
responsible sources
FSC® C020471

To find out more about our authors and books visit www.bloomsbury.com
and sign up for our newsletters

CHRIS HIGGINS

TROUBLE ON THE FARM

Illustrated by
Emily MacKenzie

AN EXCITING DAY

Bella woke up and wiggled her toes in her nice soft bed.

The early morning sun was already peeping through a gap in her curtains. From outside came the sounds of a dog barking and cows mooing.

Bella liked living in the country. She and her little brother Sid had moved there from the city with their mum and dad earlier that summer.

Leaping out of bed, she yanked open the curtains. The cows were pouring out of the field opposite and following the farmer down the lane for milking.

A boy shut the gate behind them and gently prodded the cows into line with a stick. A dog ran up and down beside him, snapping at their heels.

It was Tom and Fetch. Tom was in her class at the village school.

Bella rapped on the window but they didn't hear her. She pushed the old sash window up high and leaned out.

"See you later!" she shouted.

Tom looked up and waved, and

Fetch barked a greeting.

Bella giggled as one cow leaped high into the air away from Fetch while another jumped sideways. They looked as though they were dancing.

"Bella? Back to bed!" came Mum's tired morning voice from her bedroom. "It's not time to get up yet."

But it was. The sun was shining on the foot of her bed and the great outdoors beckoned. Bella hugged herself with excitement.

Today was Saturday and Bella and Sid were going to play with Tom and his sister Kizzy on their farm!

She couldn't wait.

★

Over breakfast Bella looked around the kitchen table and thought, *Waking up is a funny thing. Everyone does it differently.*

Especially grown-ups.

When she woke up, she was always wide awake.

When Sid woke up, he was always half asleep.

Today, Mum and Dad looked as if they were still *fast* asleep. The pair of them were sitting at the table with their chins on their hands, drinking coffee with their eyes closed and groaning a lot.

"Why are you so tired?" asked Bella.

"Working too hard," said Mum, without opening her eyes. At the same time Dad said, without opening *his* eyes, "Late night."

"Why don't you go to bed earlier?" asked Bella through a mouthful of cornflakes.

"What are we doing today?" asked Sid, who'd forgotten.

"Too many questions," moaned Mum.

"Stop crunching your cereal so loudly," whispered Dad.

Bella put down her spoon and drank her

orange juice with her eyes closed to see if:

🍃 she could

🍃 it tasted the same.

Actually, it tasted better. Then Sid tried it too and poured it all over himself, which made Mum wake up properly.

"What are we doing today?" repeated Sid patiently after he'd been mopped up. "I've got loads of energy. Look!" He thrust

his arms out and bent them at the elbow
to show off his muscles.

Well, to be honest, a space where muscles
might grow. One day.

"We're going to play on the farm!" Bella
reminded him. "Tom's mum said we could
stay all day if we wanted to."

Mum perked up. She'd forgotten about it too.

"It's lucky I remembered!" said Bella. "Come on, Sid! Let's get ready!"

She was so excited.

She'd never been on a farm in her life.

MAGDA COMES TOO

Bella got dressed quickly, but was sent back twice to change.

Mum said a pink party dress with a stiff, sticky-out petticoat and lots of frills and a fake flower in her hair wasn't a suitable outfit to play in on a farm. Neither was a onesie.

Bella kind of knew that already but thought it was worth a try.

Instead she wore a bright red T-shirt and her favourite purple leggings with stars and moons on.

Sid wanted to wear his Superman costume with the red cape. But Dad said that a cape wasn't a good idea on a farm because it might get tangled up in machinery. So he wore shorts and his dinosaur T-shirt instead.

Mum got four extra-juicy lollies with ice cream inside out of the freezer to share with Tom and Kizzy for a special treat. Then she picked a bunch of flowers from the garden for their mum.

Carefully, she wrapped the flowers up in pretty paper so they looked like they came from a posh florist's and handed

them to Bella. Sid was entrusted with the lollies, two in each hand. They were allowed to walk down the lane to the farm on their own.

Bella felt really happy as they said goodbye. She'd been looking forward to this for weeks, ever since her mum and Tom's mum, Megan, had shared a seat on the bus.

Their mums had chatted all the way home from town, aloud about playdates and Mumsnet – and in whispers about teachers and kids at school. Bella knew from experience that the whispery conversations were usually the most interesting.

Her best friend, Magda, who lived next door, was someone that they'd talked about in whispers. According to Tom's mum she was "*a force to be reckoned with*". Bella didn't know what that meant but she remembered that Mum had agreed.

As Bella and Sid walked past Magda's front door on the way to the farm, it burst open and Magda flew out, like she'd been waiting for them.

"Where are you going?" she asked.

"Tom and Kizzy's," said Bella. "I told you, remember?"

"Oh, yeah. Can I come too?"

Bella hesitated. She was pretty sure the invitation had been meant for her and Sid only, but she didn't want Magda to feel left out.

"Have you asked your mum and dad?"

"They're working." Magda's mum and dad ran a small but very popular Polish café in town and worked really hard – even on the weekend. "I know! I'll go and ask Babcia if I'm allowed."

Babcia was Magda's grandmother and she looked after her while her parents were at work. She didn't speak much English.

Bella and Sid waited patiently for Magda.

She was a long time. From inside the cottage came the sound of raised voices. (This is a polite way of saying lots of shouting.)

Sid looked at the ice lollies. "They're running down my sleeve," he said and licked the juice away. Then he did the same to his other arm.

At last Magda came out, looking triumphant.

"She says yes. Oh look, your ice lollies are melting. We'd better eat them." She helped herself to the least gloopy one and pulled off the wrapper before Bella could stop her. Sid did the same, so Bella took one too.

It's hard to eat a dripping ice lolly when you're holding a bunch of flowers. The juice ran down Bella's bright red T-shirt and she kept dropping the flowers. Some of them broke off and the ones that were left looked a bit dusty and woebegone. Magda took them off her so she could finish her lolly.

When they reached the farmhouse Magda banged on the front door. Tom and Kizzy opened it and stopped dead when they saw Magda. Behind them, their mum's eyes widened with apprehension.

"These are for you, Mrs Turnbull," said

Magda, thrusting the bedraggled bunch of flowers into her hands. She took the remaining ice lolly, which had melted right down to the stick, away from Sid and held it out to Tom and Kizzy.

"And this is for you two from Bella's mum. To share."

APPLE TREE FARM

Tom and Kizzy's farm was HUGE!

They had a good look around the farmyard first.

The farmhouse was built of the same grey granite stone as Bella's and Magda's cottages, but it was much bigger and stood proudly on its own in the farmyard. Next to it was a barn with a big red tractor in it and across the way was a row of cowsheds.

"Your house looks like a very old grandad," said Sid thoughtfully. He was right. Moss hung off the roof in big beetling eyebrows through which the bedroom windows peered like droopy, sunken eyes. A creeper had attached itself around the front door like a big hairy moustache.

Hens picked their way daintily around the farmyard, pecking at stones and straw and making funny warbling noises in their throats. Some of them were bigger and had long dribbly noses that swung from side to side as they moved.

"Ha ha! Look at those funny-looking chickens," said Sid, delighted.

"They're not chickens, they're turkeys,"

pointed out Kizzy, who was seven.

Sid laughed. "No they're not! We bought our turkey from Sainsbury's at Christmas and it didn't look like that."

"That's because its head had been chopped off and its feathers had been

plucked and it was trussed up," explained Kizzy, who had lived on a farm all her life. "The same as they do to chickens."

The smile slid off Sid's face and his mouth dropped open. "You mean ... ?" He stared at the strutting turkeys in

shock and then pointed to the busy clucking hens running around merrily in the farmyard. "When we have chicken for dinner … is that what we're eating?"

"Yes, of course. What did you think it was?"

"Chicken," he said blankly. "But I didn't know it was real chicken. I thought it was just meat."

Bella was glad Sid had said that and not her, because he was only five but she was eight and should've known better. To tell the truth, she had never really thought about what she was eating either.

Tom and Kizzy's mum, Megan, chuckled and put her hand out to Sid. "Don't worry, Sid, you're not alone. There are people much older than you that think the same."

"Yummy!" said Magda, licking her lips. "I love chicken. Chicken and chips. Chicken burgers. Chicken nuggets. I'm hungry!"

"There's lots to learn about on a farm, Sid," said Megan, ignoring her. "And the best way to do that is to explore."

"Can I drive the tractor?" said Magda, pointing to the barn.

"Whoa! Hold your horses!" said Megan in alarm.

"Have you got horses?" Magda's face shone with excitement. "Brilliant! I've always wanted to ride a horse! Bareback, standing up and in a sparkly outfit, like in the circus."

Megan bit her lip, put her hands on her hips and tried to look stern. But Bella noticed she had smiley eyes like Mum's when she was telling them off and trying not to laugh at the same time.

"I think there may be a few basic ground rules I need to go over with you first before I let you loose on my farm, Magda," said Megan. "And NOT driving tractors or riding horses bareback are two of them."

"Ohhh!" said Magda in disappointment.

"My dad wouldn't let me wear my Superman costume to your farm in case it got caught in machinery," said Sid in a small voice.

Megan dropped to her haunches and gave him a hug. "Your dad's right, but there's nothing to worry about. You've got Tom and Kizzy and your big sister to look after you."

"And me!" said Magda.

"And Magda," said Megan, doubtfully. "Tell you what, let's go inside for a drink and a biscuit and then I can tell you all about keeping safe on the farm."

"Can we have roast chicken for lunch?" asked Magda, following them into the farmhouse. "I'm starving!"

FARMS CAN BE DANGEROUS PLACES

Bella loved it in the farmhouse kitchen.
On her lap lay a fluffy bundle of purring
kitten.

Over milk and soft, warm biscuits
straight from the Aga – which was the
biggest oven Bella had ever seen in her

whole life – Megan explained all about the farm to them.

It was a bit like being at school, only cosier and sweeter-smelling. Bella kept putting her hand up by mistake to ask questions.

"Why is it called Apple Tree Farm?"

"It's been here a long time. Years ago there were lots of apple trees. Now it's a dairy farm and we keep cows instead for their milk."

"It should be called Cow Farm then," said Magda. "I like apples better than milk."

Bella shot her hand up again. "Do you milk the cows yourself?"

"No, it's all done by machinery nowadays."

"Do you make your own butter and cream?" asked Magda. "I love cream. A bit of cream would be yummy with these biscuits." She helped herself to another one.

"No, we sell all the milk."

"What about ice cream?" asked Magda hopefully.

"Afraid not. The only things I sell are flowers, pasties, fresh eggs and seasonal fruit at the farmers' market every week. I've got the last of the autumn raspberries on the go at the moment."

Then she launched at great length into the activities of the 'Milk Marketing Board and Cooperatives', which was a bit boring.

Actually, a lot boring.

Bella's eyes drooped.

Sid's head nodded.

Magda yawned out loud.

Even the kitten stopped purring and fell asleep.

"Can we go now?" asked Magda politely. "I want to look around the farm."

"Not yet. First I must warn you about *certain things* to watch out for. Farms are VERY DANGEROUS PLACES, you know," said Megan, which made Sid sit up straight.

A look of terror spread over his face as she began to talk about electric fences that would fry you and a slurry pit that would drown you in cow poo and machinery that would chop you up and spit out the pieces.

Bella thought it sounded like a horror film. She wondered how on earth Tom and Kizzy had managed to survive on the farm all these years.

"You don't need to be scared, though." Megan started to backtrack a bit when she saw Sid's face. "So long as you stick with Tom and Kizzy and watch out for the cows and keep away from water troughs and bales of silage you'll be fine. You're all sensible children."

"Magda's not," pointed out Tom.

Megan looked at her doubtfully. "Well, she will be today, won't you, Magda?"

"Yes, Mrs Turnbull." Magda nodded solemnly at her with big, innocent eyes and Megan's face softened.

"Off you go then."

Magda shot off like an arrow from a bow.

Bella hesitated at the door. She wanted to remember everything clearly and get her facts straight. "What's silage?"

"Basically, pickled grass for winter feed. It's piled up in big bales and you don't want it to fall on you." Megan smiled gently at her. "Stop worrying, Bella. I'm sure that I can trust you on my farm. Now go and have fun."

Bella stood tall. She liked Megan a lot. She reminded her of her own mum, only rounder and smilier. She would show her just how sensible and trustworthy she could be.

CHECKING OUT
THE CALVES

When Bella got outside everyone had disappeared.

"Where are you?" she shouted.

"In the barn," came Kizzy's voice.

Bella followed them inside and found them staring up at the big, shiny red tractor with its huge wheels.

"It's very clean," said Bella in surprise.

"That's because it's brand new," said Tom. "It was only delivered yesterday. It cost a bomb. Dad really wanted it but Mum says she doesn't know how we're ever going to pay for it."

"It's awesome," said Magda, her eyes shining. "Can I drive it?"

"You're not allowed!" chorused the others. Magda looked crestfallen.

"Oh yeah. I forgot."

"Come and see the cowsheds," said Kizzy to cheer her up, and she led them out of the dark barn into the sunny farmyard.

"No thanks. I don't like cows, they're smelly. What's in there?" Magda pointed to a little wooden gate in a stone wall.

"Mum's kitchen garden."

"Is that where she grows her raspberries? Can I have a look?"

Magda pushed open the gate without waiting for an answer and disappeared inside. Bella hesitated, then she and Sid followed Tom and Kizzy into a cowshed. She expected it to be covered in cow poo but it wasn't. It had nice clean straw beds for the cows, and Magda was wrong – it didn't smell. Not much anyway.

"Where are they?"

"Who?"

"The cows."

"Out in the fields. We've got calves. Do you want to see them?"

"Yes please!"

They wandered down to the field where they were kept. The calves were very curious and came up to investigate Bella and Sid, nudging them with their noses and making them laugh.

"Why are they wearing earrings?" Sid pointed to the bright green tags in their ears.

"Identification. They've got their date of birth, their mother's name, their tag number and their herd number on them." Tom sounded like a real farmer.

"What about their own name?" asked Bella.

"We know them all. This one is Usain Bolt because he's a fast runner. His mum is Flo."

"And this one is Skippy because she skips a lot. Her mum is Brenda, I think ..." Kizzy tried to read the tag but Skippy skipped away and everyone laughed.

Bella liked having the calves in a circle around her. It felt like being in the school playground.

"Do you want to see the grown-up cows?" asked Kizzy.

"Yes please!"

Tom hesitated. "Better check what Magda's up to first."

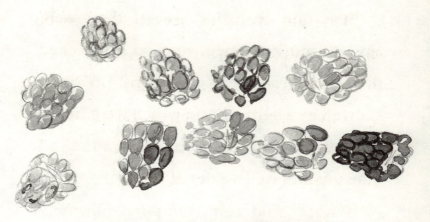

MAGDA LENDS
A HAND

They found Magda coming out of the kitchen garden with her mouth looking suspiciously red.

"What have you been up to?" asked Tom.

"Helping your mum."

"Have you been eating our raspberries?"

"Just one or two to see if they were ripe for market. They were, so I've picked them. Take some if you want!" Magda showed him her pockets, which were full to the brim with the delicious soft fruit. "And guess what else I've done!"

"What?" said Tom, sounding alarmed. Magda pointed to the wheelbarrow and Tom and Kizzy gasped. It was full of flowers.

"Oh, suffering mackerel," muttered Tom.

"Why did you pick all those?" asked Kizzy, frowning.

"For your mum," said Magda. "Hold your hands out, Bella." She tipped up the wheelbarrow and the flowers fell out into

Bella's arms. At least most of them did: the ones Bella didn't manage to catch fell on the ground. "You can give them to her if you want, because yours weren't very nice."

Bella walked into the kitchen, proudly carrying the flowers. There were so many she could hardly see over the top.

"These are for you," she said shyly, dropping a curtsey, because she'd remembered just in time that's what you do when you present flowers to someone special.

She was pleased to hear Megan give a little yelp of surprise.

"For me?" repeated Megan in a funny squeaky voice. She took them from Bella with floury hands. (Not flowery. The other flour. The one you make cakes and pastry with.)

Megan cleared her throat and tried again. "Actually, I was growing them for the farmers' market."

"Oh!" said Bella.

"Don't worry, I've picked the raspberries for you to sell instead," said Magda, and she began to pile the soft, runny fruit in a heap on the kitchen table. "Oops! Some of them have got a bit squashed."

Megan shrieked.

"Have you picked them all?"

"Pretty much," admitted Magda.

"The problem is ..." Megan closed her eyes. When she opened them she said, "The farmers' market isn't until next Friday!"

Bella stared at the flowers, which were already starting to wilt, and the pile of raspberries that were turning into a slushy, mushy mess.

Oh dear. Friday was almost a week away. Maybe this hadn't been such a good idea after all.

But Magda was still looking pleased with herself.

"We've saved you a job then, haven't we, picking all these? I can see how busy you are around here." She sniffed appreciatively. "Something smells nice. Is it roast chicken for lunch?"

"Pasties," said Megan in a strangled voice.

"Never mind," said Magda kindly. "I was hoping for roast chicken but pasties will do instead. Shall I lay the table?"

LUNCHTIME

Lunch was a bit subdued.

The pasties were delicious but Bella wasn't enjoying hers one little bit. Every time she glanced at Megan's stony face a lump appeared in her throat and she couldn't swallow.

Sid and Magda were munching away happily and didn't seem to notice, but

Tom and Kizzy looked as if they were having the same trouble as Bella. She sniffed hard and tried not to cry.

She hadn't meant to upset Megan. She loved it here on the farm. And now they'd never be invited again, even though it wasn't her fault. She hadn't picked the flowers, it was Magda. She couldn't tell Megan that though. That would be splitting on her best friend. She thought Tom or Kizzy might have said something, but they seemed to be concentrating on remaining silent and invisible.

And Bella had made it all a whole lot worse by dropping the plates. She couldn't hold on to them. When Magda had handed them to her to lay the table they were already tipping, but Megan had her back to her and didn't know that.

That was another thing she couldn't tell her.

While they were eating, Megan carried on making pasties, thumping and pounding, pulling and pummelling the pastry into shape in a way that made Bella feel slightly uneasy. Tray after tray followed each other into the oven.

"That's a lot of pasties," she observed politely.

"They're for the farmers' market!" said Megan, looking grim. "Since I'll have no fruit or flowers to sell!"

Bella felt a pang of guilt.

"You've still got eggs. I could collect

the eggs for you," offered Magda.

"NO THANK YOU!" shrieked Megan.

Magda sighed. "Can I have another pasty?" she asked.

"Why not!" said Megan, somewhat manically. "Take some home for your mum and dad for lunch, why don't you?

Oh, and don't forget your grandmother!"
She opened the oven door, grabbed a
whole tray of delicious-smelling pasties
from the shelf and slammed it down in
front of Magda.

"Thank you," said Magda, helping
herself to one and taking a big bite. "Ouch,
this is hot! Maybe I'll leave it till later. Is
there anything for afters?"

"Raspberries," said Megan darkly,
piling them into a bowl for her. "Lots of
them! Help yourself." She banged them
down in front of Magda. "And before you
ask, no, there's no cream!"

"Mmmm," said Magda through a
mouthful of raspberries. "Scrummy. By
the way, Mum and Dad are at work and

Babcia will have gone out for a walk by now, so I can stay all day. I'll take those pasties home with me for supper."

SPLAT!

After lunch the children went out to play, with strict instructions from Megan not to pick anything else to eat.

"We can't," Magda reassured her. "There's nothing left. Are you sure you don't want me to collect the eggs for you?"

"NO!" shrieked Megan. "Don't you go anywhere near those hens!"

"I won't!" promised Magda.

"And stay away from my brand new tractor!"

"I will!"

With a sigh of relief Megan flopped down in front of the TV with a pasty in one hand and a mug of tea in the other.

"Can we go and see the cows now?" asked Sid.

"Come on then, they're in the top field," said Tom, and he gave a loud whistle. "Here, Fetch!"

The Border collie came running and the children set off up the slope with Fetch leading the way, his tail wagging eagerly. Bella felt herself cheering up.

"We're going on an adventure," said Sid.

"Like the Famous Five," said Bella.

"Only we're the Famous Six!" said Kizzy. "If you count Fetch!"

"This farm is huge!" remarked Magda, surveying the lush green fields all around her. "How do you know where the cows are?"

"Easy-peasy," said Kizzy, pointing to the ground. "Follow the trail of cow pats!"

"What are cow pats?" asked Sid.

"Big splats of cow poo!" explained Tom, and everyone laughed.

"If we're going on an adventure," said Sid, "I need a stick."

Tom snapped off a thin branch from a tree and gave it to him. Immediately, Sid stuck it in a cow pat. It was hard on the

outside but soft and gooey inside, and they all stood around and said, "Yuck!"

Then they all helped themselves to sticks and stuck them in cow pats and chased each other with them. When they got tired of that they walked along the path at the side of the field, rattling their sticks against the trees and bushes.

Then they played sword fighting, till Bella put a stop to it because Sid got a bit silly.

"Use it as a walking stick," she suggested.

"Bor-ing!" complained Magda.

"OK, play golf instead."

"How do you play golf?" asked Sid.

"You hit a ball with a stick," said Bella. "You know! Grandad plays it."

"But we haven't got a ball," pointed out Kizzy.

"We could use a stone," suggested Sid.

"No, that's dangerous," warned Tom. "Somebody could get hurt."

Sid looked downcast.

"I've got a better idea," cried Magda. "Let's invent a new game. Cow pat golf!"

Sid brightened up. He liked the sound of that.

Magda took one end of her stick in both hands, pointed the other end at an impressive-looking dried-up cow pat in the sun and took careful aim. "Bella! You and me against Tom and Kizzy!"

"What about me?" shouted Sid indignantly and ran over to have a go.

"Noooooooo!" shouted Tom, but it was too late.

Magda whacked the cow pat as hard as she could and it flew up in the air and splattered.

All over Sid.

FUN ON THE FARM

Nobody had a handkerchief so they tried scrubbing poor Sid down with grass. It didn't work very well. They got it all over themselves instead.

"Yuck!" said Magda, wrinkling up her pert little nose. She rubbed her dirty hands on her thighs. "Bella, you clean him up, he's your brother. Sid, wipe your hands on Bella's leggings."

Bella looked down at her beloved moons and stars leggings and backed away from her stinky little brother. Luckily, Tom came to her rescue.

"No, Magda, it was *your* fault, you clean him up!"

But Magda didn't want to. Then she had a brainwave.

"I know! Let's have roly-poly races down the hill and it'll come off on its own."

So that's what they did, taking care to avoid the hundreds of other cow pats that lay across the field. It was like an obstacle course.

By common consent they let Sid keep winning. Again and again and again. Before long the combination of rolling in the grass and the hot sunshine had done

the trick and all the cow pat had come off.

Well, nearly all. His once-white dinosaur T-shirt was greeny-brown now, his arms, legs and face were streaked, his hair stuck out in dried-up spikes and he smelled a bit. But Sid didn't give a hoot.

He was the champion roly-polyier.

"Race you to the cows!" he shouted and tore off uphill on his sturdy little legs. Tom and Kizzy and Fetch chased after him while Bella and Magda followed more slowly behind.

Suddenly Magda came to a halt. "Is that another tractor?" she asked, peering across the field.

Bella squinted hard at the vehicle in the distance.

"I don't know. It's a bit small. Maybe it's a baby one."

"Let's take a look!"

When they got up close they could see it had much smaller wheels than the big tractor in the main barn and was a bit rusty.

It had a face. The radiator looked like a wide smiling mouth and someone had painted two cheeky eyes above it and a name beneath.

"It's called Bugsy," said Bella in delight.

Magda gazed at it longingly. "I want a go."

"You're not allowed to. Remember the rules?" Bella put her hand on her hip and wagged her finger at Magda. "*Not driving tractors or riding horses bareback are two of them!*"

"We don't even know if it *is* a tractor," said Magda.

Bella studied it. "It looks a bit like my grandad's golf buggy, only bigger."

To Bella's alarm, Magda climbed up on to it.

"Get down!"

"Why? I can drive, you know."

"Can you really?" Bella stared up at

Magda doubtfully.

"Yes. It's easy-peasy. I drove a dodgem car once at the fair."

"It's not the same!"

"Yes it is. It had two pedals on it just like this one. See? One to make it go and one to make it stop." She pushed a lever. "And this is the brake."

Before Bella's horrified eyes she pressed her foot down first on one pedal and then on the other.

Nothing happened.

"Ohhh!" complained a disappointed Magda. "I think it needs a key to start it up."

Fortunately, the key was nowhere to be seen.

THE QUARREL

Black and white cows were dotted around the top field like pieces of an unmade jigsaw puzzle.

When Bella finally managed to drag Magda away from Bugsy to catch up with the others she noticed two things:

     Cows are not half as much fun as calves.

Magda was uncommonly quiet.

The cows raised their heads to gaze at the two newcomers, then swished their tails and went back to chewing grass.

"What's the matter, Magda?" asked Kizzy, kindly.

Magda sighed. "It's boring here."

Tom and Kizzy stared at her in surprise.

"Do the cows live here or in the cowsheds?" asked Bella, showing an interest to make up for Magda's rudeness.

"Mostly outside. We move them to a different field every day."

Bella remembered waking up to the sound of mooing. "That's right! They were opposite our cottage this morning.

Why did you move them?"

"Because they ate all the grass. That's how they produce their milk."

Magda brightened up. "Can I milk a cow?"

"You don't know how to," said Tom.

"Yes I do!"

"No you don't. No one milks cows by hand any more. It's all done by machinery."

Magda stamped her foot. "It's not fair. I'm not allowed to do anything on your stupid farm!"

Tom looked cross. "Our farm's not stupid, *you* are!"

"You are! You can't even milk a cow."

"So?"

"And you can't ride a horse bareback."

"I don't want to. This is a farm, not a circus."

"And you can't drive."

"Yes I can!" said Tom, stung to the quick.

"He can!" echoed Kizzy, rushing to her brother's defence. "He can drive Bugsy, if you must know!"

"No he can't, because he'd need a key and there isn't one!" jeered Magda.

"Yes there is! It's under the driver's seat, so there!" crowed Kizzy.

To everyone's surprise Magda turned on her heel and stamped off down the field, leaving the gate wide open behind her.

"Good riddance!" yelled Kizzy.

"Shut the gate after you!" yelled Tom,

but Magda ignored them and disappeared
out of sight.

Fetch whined deep in his throat and
flopped down on the ground with his paws
over his eyes.

DON'T DRIVE A TRACTOR TILL YOU'RE OLD ENOUGH!

After Magda ran off, everyone stood still, lost in their own thoughts.

Sid slipped his hand into Bella's. He didn't like arguments.

Bella was surprised that Magda had run away. She was usually good at sticking up for herself.

Kizzy felt really guilty for upsetting Magda.

Tom frowned. Something had just occurred to him. How come Magda knew about Bugsy?

Then from down below came the unmistakeable sound of an engine starting up.

"Bugsy!" cried Tom.

"Oh no!" gasped Bella. "She's found the key!"

There was a bang and an ominous crunching noise.

"Look, it's Magda!" shouted Sid in excitement.

Above the hedge tops, Bella could make her out moving across the fields towards them. Then Bugsy chugged through the gate with Magda perched triumphantly astride it like a warrior.

"See, Bella!" she shouted above the roar of the engine. "I told you I could do it!"

Bella couldn't help thinking Magda looked magnificent. All she needed was a breastplate, a shield and a spear and she'd look like Boudicca on a chariot. Then she realised that Magda was heading straight for them!

"Jump!" yelled Tom just in time, and the four children and dog dived into the hedge.

"Sorry!" called Magda as she hurtled past. "I'm having a bit of trouble steering!

Oh flip! There's another wall coming up!"

"Left!" roared Tom.

Magda swung the steering wheel to the left and Bugsy veered sharply around towards the startled cattle. They kicked up their heels and leaped high into the air as she bore down on them.

"Right!" roared Tom.

Magda swerved the other way with the same effect. As Bugsy zigzagged his way up the field, cows scattered in all directions.

"Slow down and turn around!" yelled Tom, and Magda managed a wide, slowish circle.

"I'm getting the hang of this!" she

shouted gleefully and drove down towards them again.

Tom put his hand up like a policeman and stepped out.

"Stop!"

"How?"

"Take your foot off the right pedal and put it down on the left!"

Bella thought he sounded like Mr Smart, their teacher.

Magda did as she was told. Bugsy shuddered and came to a stop in front of them.

"That was awesome!" She jumped down,

her cheeks flushed with excitement and her hair escaping its plaits.

"Can I have a go?" asked Sid.

"No!" said Bella, gripping his hand tightly.

Tom put his hands on his hips and looked stern. "Magda, you can't just help yourself to anything you want to on a farm!"

But Magda wasn't listening.

Instead she was staring at something going on behind them.

"Uh-oh!" she said.

WHO LET THE COWS OUT?

The children turned around.

"Oh no!" gasped Bella.

The cows were pouring out of the open gate.

"Come back!" yelled Magda.

"Go get them, Fetch!" ordered Tom, and the dog shot off like a bullet from a gun.

The children followed in hot pursuit, whooping and shouting. Bella was surprised when the cows broke into a run. She'd only ever seen cows standing still.

And chewing grass

and lying down

and walking slowly

and flicking their tails

and shoving and jostling

and jumping sideways

and leaping high

and pooing.

Actually, there was a lot more to cows than she'd thought.

At first chasing the runaway cows was fun. But soon they were running so fast the children couldn't keep up.

"They're stampeding!" cried Magda.

"Stop, everyone!" shouted Tom, his arms wide. "We're making them worse!"

The children came to a halt.

Magda dropped to the ground and lay on her back, gasping for breath. "I'm dying!"

"What do we do now?" asked Bella.

Magda rolled over and scrambled to her feet. "Shall I go and get Bugsy?"

"No!" thundered Tom. "It's all your fault. You spooked them in the first place!"

"Mum told you not to drive a tractor!" Kizzy's lower lip trembled. "Now we're all going to get into trouble!"

"Don't tell her then," said Magda. "Anyway, I didn't break any rules. Bugsy's not a tractor. He's a golf buggy."

"A golf buggy?" repeated Tom. "Who said?"

"Bella."

Everyone looked at Bella.

"I said he looked a bit like one," she said sheepishly.

Tom shook his head as if he couldn't believe his ears. Bella felt very silly.

"Come on," he said. "Let's catch up with them before they do some damage."

"They can't have gone far," said Bella hopefully. "They must be in the field where Bugsy was."

But she was wrong.

The cows were nowhere to be seen.

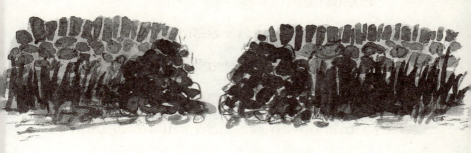

THE MYSTERIOUS CASE OF THE MISSING COWS

The cows had well and truly disappeared!

The children looked around the field in surprise.

"Where could they have got to?" asked Tom.

"They've vanished into thin air!" said Bella.

"Fizzled out!" said Magda.

"Evaporated!" said Kizzy.

"Maybe they're invisible?" suggested Sid, and he shut his eyes and stretched his hands out to see if he could feel them. "No, they're definitely not here."

Tom scratched his head. "They must be. That gate is the only way in."

Suddenly, from the far end of the field, a loud noise blasted and made them all jump. Sid flung his arms around Bella and hid his face in her tummy as more noises erupted in a humungous racket of:

hooting and tooting

honking and blaring

shouting and bawling

and angry name-calling.

"Quick!" shouted Magda, her face alight with excitement. "Let's investigate!"

The children charged across the field and came to a full stop.

"Uh-oh!" said Bella.

Now they could see the wall had collapsed just behind where Bugsy had been standing. The ground in the gap was trampled and littered with fresh cow pats.

"Oops!" said Magda, looking the teeniest bit guilty. "I didn't mean to reverse into it. Bugsy did it on his own when I started him up. Someone must've left his brake off."

Through the hole in the drystone wall a line of cars could be seen, nose to tail.

Inquisitive cows were inspecting their surprised occupants.

Tom groaned.

"I don't believe it!" he cried. "The cows have got out on to the road."

THE COWS GO ON
AN ADVENTURE

The cows were having a lovely time.

They'd followed one another through the gap in the stone wall in an orderly fashion, like people queuing to get on or off a plane. Now they were ambling along the road without a care in the world, taking in all the sights.

The traffic building up in front and behind them didn't bother them one little bit. They were far too interested in poking their heads through the windows of stationary cars and mooing hello at the people inside. Along the road they stopped to sample the many delicious plants and grasses that grew in the drystone wall, as happy as children let loose in a sweet shop.

"Good idea! Yummy blackberries!" said Magda, helping herself to the juicy fruit that was growing wild.

"Magda!" Tom glared at her indignantly as all around them car horns blasted. "This is serious! They could cause an accident and it's all your fault!"

"Sorry," said Magda indistinctly, stuffing blackberries in her mouth.

"What do you want us to do?" asked Bella.

"You and Sid pick up the stragglers and get them back into the field," ordered Tom. "And make sure you put the stones back afterwards to stop them getting out again. Kizzy and I will chase after the others with Fetch and head them off."

"What about me?" asked Magda.

"You run and tell my dad the cows are out!" said Tom.

"OK!" said Magda obligingly. "I'm a fast runner!"

"And don't forget to say whose fault it is!" he added crossly.

Magda sped off in one direction and Tom and Kizzy disappeared in the other.

Bella sighed helplessly as she and Sid were left alone. "Get them back in the field?" she repeated. "How are we supposed to do that?"

"Tom said we had to pick them up," murmured Sid, gazing doubtfully at the huge beasts. "But they're a bit big."

"I don't think he meant we literally had

to pick them up," said Bella thoughtfully. "I think we should try asking them nicely to go back home. Here, Daisy! Here, girl. This way!"

Daisy ignored her and carried on munching the top of the hedge.

"Maybe her name's not Daisy," said Sid, so they tried Brenda, Mo, Gert and Flo, but she ignored these too.

So did all the other cows.

Bella and Sid didn't know what to do. Luckily, they saw a figure flying across the field towards them. It was Magda!

"I told Tom's mum that the cows were out and it was your fault. She's gone to fetch his dad and he'll be here soon," she said.

"Why was it my fault?" asked Bella, puzzled.

"Because you told me Bugsy was a golf buggy, so I drove it and the cows stampeded," explained Magda patiently. "Haven't you got them back in yet? I'll help you."

Grabbing a stick, she went behind Daisy, who immediately moved away and turned her attention to a car's wing mirror instead, licking it with her amazingly long tongue.

"Ay up!" shouted Magda in her most commanding voice and whacked Daisy on the rump. The cow trotted off with a reproachful look.

"Don't hurt her!" cried Bella.

"I didn't, I just gave her a surprise. Cows have got tough hides," explained Magda. "Quick, head her off. Sid, you go one side, Bella, the other."

Between the three of them, they nudged, shuffled and prodded Daisy back through the gap in the wall.

The drivers who were stuck in their cars gave them a clap and got out to help them round up the rest of the stragglers, now that they saw how to do it. Before long, eight cows were safely back inside the field and the gap in the wall had been closed up with stones and branches.

But Bella noticed there were still lots of cows missing.

Strangely, even though the road was

clear again, no one seemed in a hurry to move any more. The cross drivers had mysteriously turned into jolly drivers and were high-fiving each other and saying things like "Howdy, partner!" and "I always fancied myself as a cowboy!" in pretend American accents.

But at last they got in their cars and drove away.

"Phew!" said Bella. "Now we'd better go and find the others."

THE FARMER'S ARMS

By the time they caught up with the rest of
the cows they'd travelled quite a distance.
Tom and Kizzy and Fetch had managed
to keep them on the side of the road so that
traffic could get by, but Tom was looking
worried.

"Where's my dad?" he asked.

"He's on his way," said Magda. "Bella

didn't know how to get the cows back into the field, so I had to show her. They're all tucked up safely now though."

Tom gave them both an exasperated look. Bella felt bad, like she'd let everyone down though she wasn't quite sure how.

"We need to turn this lot around to get them back to the farm," said Tom grimly. "But it's dangerous with the traffic."

Bella wanted to make amends, so she thought hard. Then she had a brainwave!

"I know how to do it safely!" she cried. "There's a pub further along the road called the Farmer's Arms. We went there for lunch last Sunday. It's got a huge car park. Let's herd the cows into it and turn them around there."

"Brilliant idea!" said Tom, and Bella felt a warm glow of happiness.

"I'll go first!" said Magda, and she smacked a cow on its rump. They set off in a long, slow, meandering line with Magda at the front, Tom and Kizzy in the middle, and Bella and Sid bringing up the rear. Fetch ran up and down snapping at the cows' heels to keep them in order.

At last they rounded a bend and the Farmer's Arms came into view. It was a big old granite pub with lots of pretty hanging baskets bursting with flowers, and today it was looking particularly festive. Bunting was fluttering in the large, empty car park and bunches of pink,

white and blue balloons were dancing in the breeze.

Magda led the way in. The cows followed, mooing appreciatively, and wandered off to explore.

Bella noticed a number of things:

A beautiful red carpet stretched from the road to the entrance, where the doors were flung wide open.

There was a table laid with buckets of champagne, rows of glasses and a massive welcome display of white lilies, roses, freesias and orchids.

A line of cars was pouring into the car park.

The last car to turn in was shiny and open-topped.

In the front was a chauffeur.

In the back were a beautiful bride and a handsome groom.

WEDDING DAY PANDEMONIUM!

Everything happened at once.

Most of the herd went straight for the pretty hanging baskets and started to chew their contents.

One cow made her way up the steps to the entrance and nibbled delicately at the display of flowers.

Bella saw, to her horror, that the red carpet was rapidly being splattered in cow poo.

And the beautiful bride and handsome groom were standing up in their open-topped car with their mouths hanging open, staring in disbelief at the herd of four-legged guests that had come, uninvited, to their wedding reception.

Oh no! They were going to get into so much trouble for this!

A man in a smart suit and a bow tie came charging out of the pub to see what was going on. By now the car park was chock-a-block with cars and cows.

"He's the Master of Ceremonies," said Magda. "Or the MC for short. You can tell by the bow tie. I know all about weddings."

First the MC shouted at the cows, who took no notice whatsoever.

Then he slapped the rump of the one who was daintily helping herself to the roses from the wedding display. Obligingly, she turned her attention to the lilies instead.

Then an elegant lady in a large hat and flouncy dress stepped out of a car straight into a fresh, ripe cow pat.

"She's the mother of the bride," said Magda knowledgeably. "They're always in pink."

Bella covered Sid's ears as the elegant lady took off her shoe and hopped about

on one leg, screeching rude words you're
not allowed to say unless you are grown
up and REALLY CROSS.

None of the cars could move, so everyone
got out. Unfortunately, the car park was
slippery now, what with so many cow

pats, and some of the guests found it hard to stay upright.

The father of the bride was the first to go down with his legs in the air, closely followed by the best man. Cleverly, he turned his embarrassing tumble into an impressive forward roll, and with a shout of "*Ta-Dah!*" got to his feet and did a big bow.

Everyone cheered and started taking photos on their phones.

Bella gasped in dismay as the three bridesmaids shrieked and grabbed each other, falling down in a heap one after the other like a row of dominoes.

One by one the guests slipped and slithered and shrieked their way across the slimy car park, most of them coming a cropper on the way.

But though everyone else had finally made it into the pub, two people flatly refused to set foot on the stinky ground.

The bride and groom.

HELP IS ON ITS WAY!

In her gorgeous white dress that looked like a fluffy meringue, and her white satin shoes, the bride said there was no way she was wading through all that muck to her wedding reception.

"Me neither," said the groom. "I hired this suit and it's got to go back to the shop tomorrow."

But the trouble was, the chauffeur couldn't drive them any closer to the pub because there were cows everywhere.

Oh no! thought Bella, trying not to cry. *Poor things. This was supposed to be the best day of their lives and now it's ruined.*

And it's all my fault.

But rescue was close at hand. At that very moment Tom and Kizzy's mum, Megan, and their dad, Jago, rode into the pub car park on a tractor.

Not Bugsy. The big red one from the farmyard.

There's something magnificent about a tractor, thought Bella in relief. *It's like a fire engine come to put things right. Or a tank. Or a chariot.*

The wedding guests must have thought so too, because they hung out of the pub windows, clapping and cheering, and the bride's mother waved her hat.

Megan and Jago leaped off the tractor and began to herd the cows into a corner of the car park, and the wedding guests came out to help. Soon people were taking selfies with the cows milling around them and everyone was laughing and joking.

Everyone except the bride and groom.

Before long the cows were safely cornered, the cars were lined up neatly to fence them in and the pub staff had rushed out with brushes and buckets of hot water to scrub the red carpet clean.

But still the bride refused to walk on it.

"It's too wet," she protested. "It'll ruin my beautiful dress."

And even though the bridesmaids said they'd hold her beautiful dress up for her, the bride couldn't be persuaded. "If I end up on my backside I'm going to look a right plonker," she said. "Look at the state of you lot!"

Bella could see her point.

The chauffeur said they could drive along the carpet, but she stamped her foot and said she didn't want to.

When her new husband tried to pick her up and carry her into the reception she whacked him over the head with her bouquet.

Nobody knew what to do.

Suddenly, Bella had a brainwave.

BELLA SAVES
THE DAY

"Excuse me," said Bella politely. "I've got an idea."

"I'm glad someone has," said the groom, who was starting to look more frazzled than handsome.

"Why don't you drive her along the red carpet on the tractor?"

The bride, who was starting to look more tearful than beautiful, paused in mid-sob.

"Are you serious? I'm not going to my wedding reception on a smelly old tractor!"

"But it's not a smelly old tractor," Bella pointed out. "It's a nice, new, shiny one. Look!"

Everyone stared at it.

It did look rather splendid in the afternoon sunshine with its high seat and huge wheels and gleaming red paint. The men were gazing at it like they'd fallen in love.

"It's brand new," confirmed Jago. "It hasn't even set foot inside a field yet."

"What a brilliant idea!" said the

groom, looking like the happiest man on the planet.

"That is so cool!" said the most glamorous bridesmaid.

"Didn't that celebrity model in *Hello* magazine go to her wedding on a tractor?" asked the bride's mother.

"Let's do it!" cried the bride, and a cheer went up around the car park.

"I'll drive you!" offered Magda but Tom, Kizzy, Sid and Bella shouted, "NO!"

"I'll drive you," said Jago.

"No, *I'll* drive you," said the chauffeur.

"*I'm* driving!" said the groom. "It's *my* wedding!"

"On your bike!" shouted the bride, climbing up into the driving seat. "This is my day!" And another cheer went up around the car park.

So Jago gave her a quick lesson, and when she was ready the guests lined up on either side of the red carpet with glasses of champagne. Then they all toasted the health of the happy couple as they chugged past them to their wedding reception at the Farmer's Arms, perched high on a tractor.

And, of course, everyone took photos of them.

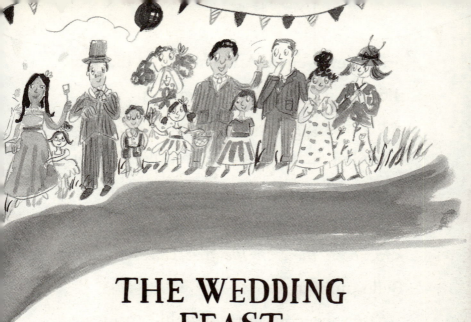

THE WEDDING FEAST

Bella and the others ended up being invited to the wedding reception. The bride's mother insisted.

"It's the least I can do. You've saved the day for us. Don't you think our Ellie looks gorgeous?"

"Beautiful!" said Megan, gazing at the

bride dewy-eyed. And she really did, now that she was happy and smiling.

"If it hadn't been for you she'd still be stranded out there in the middle of a herd of cows!" continued the bride's mother.

If it hadn't been for me the cows wouldn't have been there in the first place! thought Bella guiltily.

"But we couldn't possibly!" protested Megan. "We're not dressed for the occasion!"

"Neither are we any more!" said the bride's mother ruefully, inspecting her splattered mother-of-the-bride outfit. "Pull up a chair. We're just ready to eat. There's plenty of food to go round."

"Except for pasties," said the

bride's father, morosely. "I've got an announcement to make. The bakery has just phoned to say their oven's broken down. There will be no pasties."

"No pasties!"

Word spread around the pub like wildfire and gloom settled over the wedding guests.

"It's not a proper wedding without a Cornish pasty," said the groom's father, and there was a general murmur of agreement.

Without a word Megan stood up and walked out of the pub. A minute later Bella caught the sound of a tractor starting up.

She couldn't believe her ears. Was Megan going home because there were no pasties? What if everyone else did too?

The bride's father must have thought the same, because he clapped his hands and cleared his throat nervously.

"The buffet's open. Tuck in, everyone," he announced.

Magda got up first, closely followed by Bella, Sid, Tom, Kizzy and Fetch, who had sneaked in. Everyone else lined up behind them. It was the first wedding Bella and Sid had ever been to, unlike Magda, who was an old hand.

"You don't have to take everything now," explained Magda, doling out the plates. "You can keep

going back for more."

Bella chose a cheese straw with avocado dip, a canapé, which was a small piece of toast with a weird thing on top, and a cupcake.

Sid chose a sandwich, crisps and two cupcakes.

Magda chose five crab cakes, four cocktail sausages, three roast potatoes, two giant prawns on a stick and one vegetable tartlet. And three cupcakes.

"It looks yummy," she said, examining her heaped-up plate. "Pity there are no pasties to finish it off."

And that seemed to be the general consensus of the wedding guests as they devoured the delicious buffet.

Then ...

... lo and behold!

The door opened and Megan walked in proudly bearing a tray piled high with pasties.

TIME TO GO HOME

The pasties had all been consumed and pronounced much better than the bakery's.

The buffet had been devoured, bar the odd courgette canapé and a few fishy bites.

Glasses had been refilled and the health and happiness of the bride and groom had been toasted. Loads.

Speeches had been made in which cows and pasties featured prominently and to great hilarity.

Tables and chairs had been moved to one side and a space had been cleared ready for dancing.

"Weddings are all the same," said Magda, yawning, as some guests began to make their way to the bar while others drifted on to the dance floor. "You eat a lot, drink a lot, talk a lot and dance a lot."

"Is that all?" asked Sid.

"Yeah. Pretty much. They get a bit boring after a while. Can we go home now?"

"Shame! I was just fancying a quick

twirl," said Jago, grabbing Megan around the waist. She brushed his hand away.

"Time to go," she said. "Their parents will be wondering where they've got to."

Outside, Magda asked hopefully, "Can I ride home on the tractor?"

"No," said Megan, "you can walk," and she climbed up beside Jago. "I'm off home to put the kettle on. I need a cup of tea after all that champagne."

The children and Fetch set off down the road after the tractor, following the trail of dried-up cow pats back to the farm. Now all the excitement was over, Bella was starting to get worried. Megan had seemed a bit grumpy.

The closer they got to the farmhouse, the more nervous Bella became.

She was pretty sure they were going to be in trouble. True, the day had panned out well in the end. But when all was said and done, Magda had:

picked Megan's flowers

eaten her raspberries

driven her tractor

knocked down her wall

and let her cows escape.

Bella knew from experience that when Magda got into trouble, she did too. And, to be fair, it had been Bella's idea to herd the cows into the Farmer's Arms car park.

When they reached the farmhouse Tom

and Kizzy asked them in.

"No thank you," said Bella quickly. "We'd better get home."

"Ohhhh!" said Sid in disappointment. Then he ran on ahead up the lane.

"See you tomorrow!" called Magda cheerily as she opened her gate. "Shame Megan gave all the pasties away, I'm starving! I wonder what's for dinner?"

Mum was at the front door looking out for Bella.

"What have you been up to?" she said. "Sid's been telling us a fine tale. Something about the cows getting out and you chasing them along the road."

Bella's heart sank.

Inside the house Sid was in full flow and

it was too late to stop him. "And the cows ate all the flowers in the pub car park."

"Really?" asked Dad. "Not the Farmer's Arms?"

Sid nodded enthusiastically. "Yes! There was a wedding on and the cows pooed everywhere and the bride cried."

Dad burst out laughing.

Mum looked alarmed. "That's our local! Please tell me this isn't true!"

"It is true! It is!" said Sid, jumping up and down to prove his point. "Everyone fell down and got poo on their clothes."

Dad gave a big belly laugh and fell about, clutching his sides.

Mum groaned. "How did the cows end up in the pub car park?"

"Bella told us to put them there."

Mum's eyes grew big as footballs.

"Bella? You and I need to have a serious word."

AND THE CONSEQUENCES WERE ...

Bella woke up and wiggled her toes in her nice warm bed.

Then she remembered.

Last night Mum had had a serious word with her. Lots of serious words.

Words like: *responsible* and *sensible* and *trustworthy* and *mature* and *dependable*.

And how she hadn't been any of them.

Bella had tried to explain to her that she had, but Mum wasn't listening. Instead she'd sent her to bed *to reflect on the consequences of her actions*, which is what she always did when she thought Bella had been naughty.

Bella had felt really sad. She'd done as she was told and got as far as two consequences before she'd fallen asleep. (Well, it had been a very busy day.)

But thinking about them now made her sad all over again.

She wouldn't be allowed to play on the farm any more. And mums would have those whispered conversations about her like they did about Magda.

Bella sighed. It could've been worse. It was only Sid's story. And as Megan hadn't come round to complain maybe they would think he was making it up.

Bella got washed and dressed and went downstairs, where everyone was having a quiet breakfast.

Very quiet.

"Can I play with Magda today?" she asked.

"No," said Mum from behind the newspaper.

It was going to be one of those days, she could tell. There was no point in asking if she could play with Tom and Kizzy because she already knew the answer to that.

Bella helped herself to cornflakes, and then she and Sid made themselves scarce.

First they switched on the TV. After a while Mum came in and told them to switch it off and go out and play in the sunshine.

They went out to the back garden, where Sid dug for treasure with a stick. Then they made an adventure playground for the ants he'd disturbed, out of sticks and stones and leaves and a seagull's feather.

When they got bored with that they moved to their front garden.

"There's nothing to do!" moaned Bella.

"Come up here!" came a voice. It was Magda, so high up in the big sprawling tree that took up almost the whole of her front garden that she couldn't be seen.

"We can't."

"Why not?"

"We're not allowed to play with you today."

"We don't have to play," said Magda. "We can talk."

It would be a great place to keep out of Mum's way. Bella and Sid slipped into her garden and climbed up beside her.

"What shall we talk about?" asked Bella, but they couldn't think of anything.

"I know! Let's tell each other jokes instead," suggested Magda, so they did. Only Sid made his up and they got sillier and sillier, which made them laugh even more.

Then Bella heard voices and put her finger to her lips.

Tom and Kizzy were coming up the lane. With their mum!

To Bella's horror they turned in at her gate and rang the doorbell. She could hear the front door opening and Mum's surprised voice inviting them in.

Oh no! Now she was for it!

... BELLA WINS
THE DAY

"BELLA! Get down from that tree and come inside immediately!"

When she heard Mum calling her, Bella knew it was time to face the music.

"I'll come with you, Bella," said Sid, loyally.

"So will I," said Magda, and they

clambered down from their hiding place.

When they went in everyone was looking very serious and solemn.

But then to Bella's surprise, Kizzy let out a giggle and everyone burst out

laughing. "What's happened?" asked
Bella, bewildered.

"Where do I begin?" laughed Megan.
"The phone hasn't stopped ringing all
morning!

"Number one – I've got a contract from the Farmer's Arms to provide all their pasties from now on. They liked mine so much they want me to supply them on a permanent basis.

"Number two – another contract for plants to fill their hanging baskets."

"So long as we keep our cows away from them!" interrupted Kizzy.

"And … best of all …" announced Tom. "Number three – we've had loads of requests for the hire of our new tractor for weddings!"

"At a ridiculously high price, I might add," said Megan, her eyes shining.

"The wedding guests posted their photographs," explained Tom. "Now it's all gone viral on social media."

"And everyone wants to go to their wedding on a tractor!"

Dad whipped out his smart phone. "Flipping heck! I see what you mean!"

"And from what Tom and Kizzy tell me, Bella, we've got you to thank," cried Megan.

"How come?" Bella was baffled.

"You were the one who had the sense to move the cows into the pub car park."

"I was the one who let them out in the first place!" said Magda.

"But it was Bella who suggested using the tractor to drive the bride and groom to their wedding reception," pointed out Megan. "So it's all down to her."

Megan beamed at her and Mum did too.

"I think I owe you an apology, Bella," smiled Mum.

"And you owe me one too!" piped up Sid. "I *told* you it was true."

ACKNOWLEDGEMENTS

Thanks to Naomi for
telling me all about life
on your amazing farm
CH

Find out how Bella and Magda
first met in

TROUBLE NEXT DOOR

AVAILABLE NOW
Read on for a sneak peek!

A NICE SURPRISE

Bella was sitting on the front doorstep feeling grumpy.

It wasn't fair. She'd told Sid there was a ghost in their attic and he wanted to see it. But Mum said there was nothing there and they should go out to play, even though she'd *promised* they would look for it in the morning.

Mum and Dad were really busy. Dad was laying a new carpet in the living room and Mum was scrubbing and polishing every available surface.

Bella was bored. It was all right for Sid. He was happy poking a stick around in the earth but Bella didn't know what to do. She wished she had someone to play with.

"Hello," said a voice, and she looked around. There was no one to be seen. "Hell-o-o!" persisted the voice. "I'm here!"

Bella and
Sid sprang to
their feet. The voice
seemed to be coming
from the cottage next door.
But when they peered over the wall
there was nobody there. Just a messy
garden with a jumble of wild flowers
and grass and a big, sprawling tree,
thick with leaves.

O-O-O!

O-O!

"Look up!"
commanded the voice.
It was coming from
high up in the tree.

Two bare legs
appeared,
then a pair of dusty
pink shorts,

a rather grubby
white T-shirt with a
mermaid on it and,
finally, a head.

A girl dangled
from a branch for
a second, arms
outstretched,

then she raised her legs and started swinging, higher and higher. Suddenly, she launched herself into the air, did a backward somersault and landed the right way up, arms straight, like a gymnast.

"Wow!" said Bella.

"Wow!" said Sid.

"Hello," she repeated, dusting herself down. "I'm Magda."

"I'm Bella and this is Sid," replied Bella. Then she remembered her manners. "How do you do?"

"How do I do what?" asked Magda. Her voice sounded different.

"That's what you say to be polite," said Bella.

The children examined each other curiously.

Bella thought that she would like to have long fair plaits and bright blue eyes like Magda.

"I like your plaits," she said.

"I like your curls," replied Magda. "And his." She pointed to Sid.

Sid grinned at Magda. "I'm five," he said. "How old are you?"

"Eight."

"I'm eight too," said Bella, pleased.

"Twins!" said Magda, and Bella was even more pleased.

"Do you live here?" she asked.

"I do now," said Magda. "I used to live in Poland."

"Where's that?"

Magda shrugged. "A long way away."

"I used to live a long way away too," said Bella sadly. "I don't know anybody here."

"You know me," said Magda. "Can I come and play in your back garden? It's got raspberries in it."